Pitschi

The kitten who always wanted to be something else.
A sad story, but one which ends well.

by Hans Fischer

Harcourt, Brace & World, Inc., New York

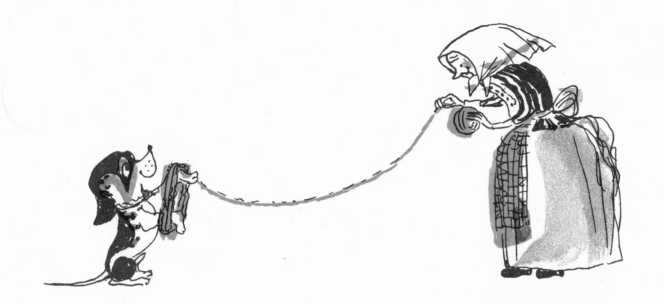

OLD Lisette is sitting in front of her house knitting. Near her on the bench sleep the two cats, Mauli and Ruli. They have five kittens who are just six weeks old. The two who are wrestling together are Grigri and Groggi. The one who has caught hold of the ball of wool is called Patschi, and the one who is trying to climb up the broom is Mitzi. One more, the smallest and the nicest of them all, does not play like the others. He stays in the basket and dreams. He is Pitschi. The good dog, Bello, looks at him thoughtfully. He is worried because Pitschi does not want to play.

And now Lisette gets up and goes into the kitchen. Bello trots along with her. While Mauli and Ruli keep on sleeping peacefully, Grigri, Groggi, Patschi and Mitzi grow bolder. They catch hold of Lisette's knitting, play with it and pull it every which-way. They knock down the broom and climb over it merrily. Only Pitschi doesn't find that amusing and he even goes away from the house. He wants something entirely different.

Lisette owns other animals. Behind the house are the little chickens with whom Pitschi would like to play. But the mother hen will have none of this. She calls all her children together and goes off with them. This startles Father Rooster, but when he sees that it's only a small kitten, he turns around. How proudly he walks away.

"I would like to be a proud rooster," Pitschi thinks, and he struts along behind him. He does very well on two legs. He learns to peck also, and he can soon crow almost as well as the big rooster. Each one tries to crow more loudly than the other.

But this makes a neighboring rooster angry. And a regular cockfight begins. "Oh no, if that's the way it is, I don't want to be a rooster!" cries Pitschi, and in a great fright he runs away—far into the meadow. There lies a brown animal—a large one—but he seems very gentle. He is Lisette's goat.

"I would like to play that I'm a goat," says Pitschi. So the gentle goat brings Pitschi the bell that he wears on Sundays. Pitschi breaks off two twigs to use for horns. He holds them to his head and asks, "Now, don't I look just like you?" "Yes indeed," answers the goat.

Then Lisette arrives to milk the goat. "I don't want to be milked!" miaows Pitschi and runs away frightened.

But Pitschi soon makes a new acquaintance. This time it is a duck. She is busy cleaning her feathers. "I can do that as well as you can," thinks Pitschi and he licks himself. "I believe I'm a duck." And he waddles along, like the other ducks, to the pond. The ducks go into the water one after the other and swim away. That looks easy, and Pitschi wants to try it too.

But oh my! Pitschi sinks down, of course, and he would surely have drowned if a clever duck had not saved him. See how she dives! With the kitten on her back she comes up again. He lies between her wings as though he were in a little boat, and the duck carries him to the shore. Mother Rabbit and her little ones look on astonished.

The little rabbits grow more and more friendly. They sniff Pitschi's whiskers with their warm noses. Pitschi stands still and is happy. ''If my ears would only grow a little, I would be a rabbit too,'' he thinks.

The ducks swim away again. The rabbits come closer to Pitschi, but not too close, for he is dripping wet. They wait until he dries off a bit.

Evening is coming. Mother Rabbit claps her hands and calls, ''Run home quickly. It is bedtime.''
The little rabbits are obedient and their mother doesn't have to call them twice. And because
Pitschi thinks he is a rabbit, too, he jumps into the cage with them.

When it is dark, Lisette shuts all the cages so that no bad animals can get in during the night. She shuts the rabbit cage, but she does not know that Pitschi is inside! The kitten has crouched down between two rabbits because he is freezing after his cold bath in the pond. And soon, dead tired, he falls asleep. In the middle of the night, Pitschi wakes up. He doesn't know where he is. He wants to go home to Lisette. Then he realizes that he is locked up in a wire cage and he begins to cry, ''Miaow, miaow!'' The moon comes out and Pitschi sees dark animals from the forest coming toward the cage. They come nearer and nearer—right up to the wire! The fox opens its mouth wide, and the owl makes wicked, angry eyes. Pitschi is dreadfully afraid and he cries louder and louder. Will no one in the house hear him?

At last Bello hears him. He barks until Lisette wakes up. She turns on the light and opens the window. The bad animals are afraid of the light and they run away. Bello jumps out of the window and barks at them. Then he hunts for Pitschi and because he has a good sense of smell, he soon finds him. Pitschi isn't crying any more, he is half dead of fright.

Lisette carries Pitschi home.

She rubs him dry and wraps him up warmly.

Then she tries to give Pitschi some milk. And look, he's really drinking it! Lisette is happy.

Next morning, Pitschi is very sick. The door opens, and all the animals come to visit Pitschi.

You can see how much they like him. The little kittens aren't playing any more. Everyone is sad.

Each day Pitschi gets better. But he is still very weak. Then Bello has a good idea. He builds a small wagon from the cats' basket. Father Mauli brings Lisette's parasol to put over the carriage, and Mother Ruli fetches a soft cushion.

Pitschi is allowed to go out. But he is still sad for he cannot forget that terrible night. All the animals want Pitschi to laugh again so they plan something very gay. They will give a big party in Lisette's flower garden. Mauli, Ruli and Bello take Pitschi there.

Now the party is over. Only the little kittens cannot stop playing and dancing. Pitschi plays happily with them. From now on he doesn't want to be anything but a kitten. His favorite game is Cat and Mouse.

Meanwhile Lisette has prepared a surprise. She calls, "Wash your hands and come to the table. There is something good."

Bello carries in the surprise. It is a mountain of whipped cream with ladyfingers. Pitschi has a cushion behind his back. He is still being pampered a bit. He looks at Lisette and thinks: "What a good, sweet woman! I'll never leave her again. This is the best place after all."